AF449079

THE SWEET WORDS THAT HURT US BOTH

∞

Xei R. M.

A Collection of Poetry and Prose

Published by:

CENTRAL BOOKS SUPPLY, INC.
927 Phoenix Bldg., Quezon Ave.,
Quezon City
www.central.com.ph

ISBN: 978-621-02-0942-6

Cover design by GELO MANALILI
Illustrations by ALEX AGUINALDO

Preface

Remember the person who you thought would stay with you for long—but didn't? Imagine if your relationship was a reverse... if it started with mess and tears, and ended right when you had all the butterflies in your stomach?

This book is the same. Defying the order of time.

Initially, this was following the normal love sequence, first—"the sweet words." It is when you fell in love with each other because everything you said and did were perfectly fit puzzles. Next, "that hurt us both" when you both chose to leave because puzzles do not fit anymore. When I had written three related poetry about the pain of losing someone, the depression, and the freedom from being in chain, it stressed me to think of how to situate them in the book. So, I sacrificed the whole book for those poems, but I am glad that the idea turned up on me. I was actually at the brink of considering this part as an "afterword" or "postface" because of its supposed-to-be format.

I have written this book because I could not let these emotions and thoughts, which helped me to just vanish. When you read poetry, watch movies, listen to music and its lyrics, look at the landscape, stare at the night sky, or think of the person you like, words will simply pop out of your mind waiting for you to be written down. You have to write it because it is beautiful; both the process and the product of putting words together.

I want to share this with you all because like people, books can change lives too. This book contains the emotions we feel which we are afraid to turn into words and tell to those we love or loved, to our own selves, and to the stars we choose to reach or to just stare at.

I want to thank all my friends, cousins, and my family who have supported me and given me their opinions about my writings; especially to Gelo, for designing the cover page, and Alex for his illustrations, to Miss Roann for checking on my poems and for sharing her thoughts and time with me, and to my sister as well for the copy read.

To readers, thanks a lot! You know, I have just
realized how difficult it is to make a book. Man, it
is no joke.

Xei R. M.

The Sweet Words that Hurt us Both

It's terrible how you started as Rose and Jack
but ended like Titanic.

Those *good mornings*
when we're not really happy upon waking up.
Those *good nights*
when we weren't truly sleepy.
Those *I miss yous*
when we were merely sad.
Those *I love yous*
when we only have liked each other.
Those are

      the sweet words
        that hurt us both.

It's a paradox
that we spent too much money on studying
and yet, we never actually learned.

Perhaps, the reason
why history tends to repeat itself
is because we go back to our past very often.

It won't be surprising
if the future we try to look forward to is...
but a saddening time machine.

Warring Emotions and States.

I remember how much you killed me—
when you left.

It felt like my organs
were failing one after another
as the sound of your footsteps
r e c e d   e   s   .

FALLING IN REVERSE

How I wish our relationship started full
of pain and regrets
that we have to curse each other
and hope we didn't meet.

Followed by countless, endless fights,
questioning us,
questioning the world we are in, and
questioning God for what is happening.
Blaming myself for the things I shouldn't have done
and you for walking away.

Comes next
is the period before all the problems even existed.
When people are wishing us a stronger bond,
and when they are yet to learn that we are dating.

Then, the point when we fell so in love.
When we talked about our deepest,
metaphysical thoughts in every exploration
or while we are sitting under the stars.
The phase when we started to explore

our personal secrets, behind our fitted clothes
and our oily foreheads.
The stage when I first introduced you
to my family and me to yours.

After those were the dates:
We had our first kiss on the third
and my heart pounded uncontrollably,
like when several hundreds of meteors
crash into the Earth's surface,
one after the other in just a minute,

On our second rendezvous,
when I was so preoccupied with the thought
of telling you how much I like you,

On the first date,
when we let ourselves lose in a party
and we were so happy talking about our lives
as we introduced ourselves to each other,

The first time we met,
when you smiled at me
like I've forgotten my name
or who I was for a second.

And that intense final moment
when you first appeared before my eyes
like the scene when the sun
is about to touch the horizon at dawn
and the world is stunned
for its overwhelming beauty.

If this occurs in our relationship,
I would undoubtedly and definitely
spend every millisecond of my life
dreaming of meeting you again,
for an extremely exciting ending.

I'm glad that I don't worry about you anymore.
But guess what?
I think that you still need it.
My care.
And I'm saying this,
Not because I want to be with you again.
You never asked me to stay.
I think am just proud of my past self.
Nothing more.
Nothing less.

Looking at the stars,
he knew he was staring at a distant past.
While the migration of the first men are taking place;
While the Great Pyramids are being built;
While a good portion of Asia
are being conquered by Alexander the Great;
While gladiators are fighting in a pit;
While the coronation of Charlemagne is being held;
While the whole Europe
is suffering from the Black Plague;
While da Vinci's preparing to paint;
While Savery's inventing the first steam engine;
And while the Second World War
has come to an end—

While those important events
were all happening in the midst of his weary eyelids...
a flash of one heartbreaking scene of him
losing a great part of his being quivered him.
Leaving the man in wonder if
he will see her again.

You are all my tragedy and euphoria

at this very moment
I am having a catharsis.

If Mars were a habitable planet, I would certainly leave the Earth now.

I want to see the Ginkgo leaves fall from its branches when the summer is gone.

If I own a kite, I'll surely let it go with the wind.

I want to forget you. I want to burn your room in my heart, but I cannot. I miss you so much that I want to see you again even if it hurts. I miss your kiss every time we part ways. I miss how beautiful you look in any way you tie your curly hair. I miss your cute look when you eat ice cream, you would slowly pull the spoon out of your mouth while your nose is pinched. I miss the way you hold my hand even if you would always say that it's ugly and rough, you still love it and you feel warm when it's close to you.

Yes, I do miss you! I wonder if you miss me too.

You know how it feels when you are about to leave someone who mean the world to you? You utterly want to stay, but you no longer understand the concept of the world you used to enjoy.

Yes, you love the person so much. You gave your best. You saw it all. And now, you have no other choice except of letting go.

It only sucks because it's coming from you.

Our future isn't predetermined so our fate depends on how great we are doing in the present. It's true that we're in love with each other today, but tomorrow is unsure whether we'll still be or become strangers again. We might end up like that in fairytale stories or dystopian novels.

If I die today,
I want my remains to be thrown to the sea.
So that you have a place to go when you are down.

I want your eyes set on me.
Your tears fall on me.
Your knees down on me.
Your body resting on me.

I'll be there.
I promise!
Just cry, baby.
Let it all out.

I'll hold you close.
I'll bear your sadness.
I'll wrap your body

like I always did
before, when we're asleep.

It was me who came first.
I pushed myself so hard
towards your already complicated life.

Forgive me!
It was entirely my fault.
I pulled you into an even more chaotic world.

In two hours of sitting here in this cold night,
I couldn't finger-count how many planes
have passed and gone by minute after minute.

I hope broken feelings arrive
and leave just the same.

But you know when I was in love?
It felt like *I was*
there on every plane...

flying.

You were the happiest among couple. You had set out
in a bay against the rising sun, complete with things
essential for the high seas: food, water, clothes and
anything else that may satisfy your need. You even
brought fishing rods so you could fish together.
You've witnessed islands of varying forms and beauty.

Throughout your journey, several storms have passed
but you've made it through. Until, after traversing
four wide oceans and six dangerous seas, you decided
to dock first in a harbor before the bleeding sunset...
and you never saw each other again.

DREAMS

I let you go because of dreams.

Just as every couple,
we had plans too.
When we ran out of topic,
we talk about them—
travels, investments, home, kids.
I loved it when you look at me in the eye
and express what you want to have
with me in the years to come.

But within those months
in no great shakes kind of reasons,
we would mean to ignore each other
until one of us eats his pride.
A sly sorry missing of emotions.
Exhausted only for some lovely days.
Then fight again.

The succeeding years,
our dreams become nightmares.
We traveled to the wrong places.
We invested in wrong decisions.

We built a home on a quicksand.
And we gave birth to many monsters.

Yet, I told you not to give up.
One night, you had a bad dream;
and in the other nights it followed,
things were breaking in your sleep.
You said that those were the signs.

Still, I didn't accept any of it.
On the contrary, I gave you flowers.
I gave you chocolates.
I cheered you up.
I never told you,
that while you tried to decipher things
incorrectly every night,
I dreamt of your death;
and in every waking moment,
I loved you even more.
I reminded you of how we started.
How I appreciated your beauty,
your being,
your messy hair,
the freckles on your skin.
I know it may not happen anytime soon.

But dreaming of your passing made me realize
how miserable I can be when you're gone.

Despite everything,
you didn't change how you think.
At all!
You just kept going.

But I tried to understand
that our dreams can take us forward too.
So I let you go.

TERRIBLE THINGS.1

You actually had a good start
You knew that you had a feeling for each other.
Your connection grew strong.
You were able to escape from the civil war.
You were able to swim through this drowning life.
Yet, still, you ended up beneath the ocean.
Separated.
You been wondering what happened.

It's terrible, isn't it?
How you started as Rose and Jack,
But ended like Titanic.

I hate love for it is forcing me to hate everything I showed love to. I love to read but you appear in every character I'm supposed to admire. I love to drink but you'd only become my hallucinations. I love to dream but I couldn't close my eyes because the moment I do, you are all I'd see.

Why can such a lovable woman make a loving man to be so hateful of her?

I hate how love can be both a requirement to be with someone and a prerequisite to be alone in the end.

You are Romeo and Juliet
without poisons and potions involved;
and so you both lived,
but still separately ever after.

We were listening to Paramore songs when we let ourselves lose in the air. We were on top of our lungs singing, as if we were on the ground before the stage they were performing at. We became the guitarist, the drummer and Hayley herself. We were jumping and screaming while smashing ourselves with pillows and bathing with cottons from inside of them. We painted the room red in harmony with their music. We were so in love, and with everything in the room—the things we were seeing and those songs we were listening to.

I felt the nostalgia being in that place again after several years. I took my phone out and browsed the playlist I was treasuring for a very long time and listened to it. While in tears I laughed—we have never even made it to their concert together.

CONGRATULATIONS...
I MISSED YOU!

If I could turn back time, I won't go further and start our relationship all over again. It was great. It was the best. It was almost perfect; until I let you walked away, crying. That last second before you disappeared completely in my sight, it is all that I need—I could have made up with you, caged you in my arms and never let you go. I should have pictured how hurtful it was on your end. I should have been better for you. I should have been calling you those final nights after work to check how you were doing, whether you were fine or troubled. I should have been asking what you were thinking. I should have comforted you. I should have wiped your tears and lifted you up when you were feeling down. I should have hugged and kissed you when you were about to give up. I made a huge mistake, and I know that saying sorry will never be enough nor will it ever be possible now.

Had I gone back to that very moment, I would have been the one receiving your "good mornings" and "goodbye kisses" now. I would have been the one you're sharing dreams with late at night. More importantly, I would have been the reason you're wearing that fancy ring people keep asking you about.

I know that he loves you; so much as you have loved me. You would have never said 'yes' when he knelt down if we're the same.

What if I was wrong to walk away?
What if you see me the way I see you?
What if you do love me
and just waiting for me to make the first move?

But it seems that
I was the only one on the see-saw.

Still, what if it was true?
What if I took the risk?

Perhaps it would hurt me less
than thinking of these at every 3 a.m.
and I couldn't sleep.

I already killed you in my dreams.
You died that moment you chose to leave.

Though mourning took me years,
I'm a different person now.

I'm capable of killing people with the very knife
They put into my heart.

"I'm sorry if I walked away. I really do! Sorry for leaving all of our problems to your hands when I should've been the one carrying them. I couldn't even picture how bad you were hurting then. It wasn't right for me to leave, but I still did. I tried to find myself in every place that I went, but never succeeded. I always failed. Until now that you're here and I'm seeing you again. It's so familiar; this is the exact same atmosphere I had when I first met you. This and your absence is clearly the reason I wander. It's certainly you who I was trying to find. I know this is too cliché, but if second chances are real," he looked at her with sincerest eyes and asked, "Will you love me again?"

There are things we just can't allow to happen twice
in our lives.

You don't want to accept the same person who
brought the Bubonic Plague across three continents
seven centuries ago.

GRAVITY

Never hope that someday
when our paths cross again,
I'll come back to you as a moon
and flood your broken city
with the tides of my love.
Because it is clear as the water
that the Earth itself
was the first to let go of the moon
By destroying the only thing
that pulls them together—
gravity.

I'm the guava tree you'd only seek
    when you are wounded
    and in need of my leaves to treat it.

When all along
    you've been eating an apple a day,
    thinking it makes you healthy.

I have no idea how deeply I fell for you until you said,
"Let's stop." I thought I could stand it so I told you
that, "it's ok". Yet, I could not. I could not! I know that
you are here deep inside my mind controlling my
neurons. When I try to look at objects, they're blurry.
When I try to hear sounds, they're simply buzzing.
Your existence and laughter are the only things my
mind and my heart accept and desire.

I said it's fine, but you're right, it really is not.

She said she loves me
to the moon and back.
One night, it was so dark
I couldn't find her anywhere.

I've waited for months and still,
there are no news about moon-landing
nor rockets going up there.

Please tell me.
Tell me the things you don't like.
The unpleasant things you're keeping since
you were a child.
The situations you've been hurt badly
but people laughed at you nonetheless.
Tell me what was running on your mind each moment
you see your dad hurting your mom.

I want to know your thoughts every time we make love.
It's way deeper than I could ever reach.

You see, I can't love the entirety of your home
when I am only welcome in the living room.
I know that you're hiding scars.
I could hear crawls behind the ceiling when we talk.
I could hear the trusses creak when the wind blows.

You are scared, I know.
When our fingers entwined, you hold my hand so tight
like you are always going to be lost in the place.
You are afraid to release those demons,
as if I am a man from the heaven myself.

I wish it could be as easy
as how your tongue reach for mine when we kiss.

You said you just wanted to pass by
    to see how I was doing.
But you left my room worse
    than the moment you have entered.

How many times have I told you that I love you? That
I was willing to paint the skies for you? That I didn't
mind swimming or diving with the deep-sea creatures
inside your head?

For so long you've been looking for a person who
won't hurt you but rather show you the meaning of
home, someone who won't mind sitting beside you on
a bench through the night under the pouring rain.

Then there was I, kneeling before you, offering the
Titanic that Rose and Jack once filled with their love
and affection.

However, while I was trying my best to save the ship
from sinking, you were there busy hammering the
portside to widen the hole.

And congratulations it sank!

So I decided to walk away, packed my things, flew
for Tibet and climbed the Mt. Everest.

Then now, after a very tough, dangerous, long
journey, you have come to me presenting your
hands, telling me you want to hold mine.
Unfortunately, these very hands are already frozen
and you won't feel anything anymore, but mere
coldness.

Now that you're completely gone, I won't expect for you to return. You have never even risked yourself to look back at me after every goodbye when we were still together. It is the reason why I really hated you going, because it always... always felt like you'd never come back.

You will never come back!

I know that
	everything fades.

Love
	fades.

You were just the first
	to feel it.

Don't blame me if I love you too much.
You deserve it.

I know I don't deserve this,
but you were the only smile I know.
It's been a long time since,
yet the wounds were so deep—
they never abandoned me in this pit as you did.
I drowned in sadness that
I learned to breathe down here.

How does it feel like to be happy, again?

A SONG FROM THE PAST

In the future, these children will sing a song to their offspring about the battle you've won here and how well you've fought against me. How greatly you stabbed my heart in front of me. It would be passed on from generation to generation while I remain lying down here on my grave, in silence, *still holding my wound.*

Pain and happiness both sail through my veins. Sometimes, I'm aboard the ship of the latter. Sometimes, with the former. And it's strange that with the entire journey I have taken so far, I had more adventures with pain than happiness. Perhaps it is why you often see me active, because I am sailing with it.

It's been a year now.
But I can still feel your arms wrapped around me,
your scent that lingered in the air
and your tears on my shoulders.

You were still the person I hugged the last time.

You were once a part of my dream,
but now, of my memory.

I never realized until this time,
that future could happen first
before the past.

That is why I couldn't fill your emptiness, because it's actually full of someone else. You are the brightest thing in my room and as I go to the next picture, then the next and the next—you are far better when I am gone. While I feel worse since I left.

I'm lost.
Days of no communication and I'm already lost.
I couldn't think of anything but only you.

I've been everywhere.
Yet, I still couldn't find you.
You were just there before.
Your being fill every space my
mind falls into, my
heart falls into.

Now, I can't move my feet well.
I can't eat well.
My body feels so hopeless,
for you are the very energy it needs.
Please go home.
Those places are missing you so.

I still remember how happy you were that moment when I brought you a gift—a dress you absolutely loved. For months, I have been trying to save money to buy it.

It was worth it! That was the only piece of clothing you wore that day.

I miss you! I miss everything about you. Your smile, your movement, your reactions, and your voice— you were so damn sexy! You're a star, truly. You're a star that still shines in the sky even after death. I want to see and feel you again. I want to live a life full of bliss with you, again.

I can still see you behind
every word I write.

   Tonight,
I won't stop writing until
   my pen runs out of ink.

2 2 2

2 days.
I'm starting to hate the clock when it rings,
It is as if a wailing siren
Like there's fire in the neighborhood.
Actually, there's no longer fire at home.

2 weeks.
I walk through the heavy rain—
Through the gloomy realization that, after all,
Butterflies are just a collective museum display.
Pinned. Frozen in a place for my own viewing.

2 months.
I drink each night—
Tequila, beer and whiskey.
They all turn up to me as if I am fucking empty.

Well, I kind of forget you.
Until I go out of the bar.
Again, and again, I miss the train.
Again, and again, I miss you dear.

You had my soul when you left,
and this body suffered too much.

Until now
that it finally found its way back to me.

I feel better and lighter than ever...
yet, I love you still.

Maybe it was the rightest thing for us to do—to
part ways. Our relationship wasn't healthy anymore;
we were taking in the dirtiest oxygen and it felt so
hard to breathe. At least, now that I'm here and
you're away, we get to exhale clean air.

Sometimes, it is impossible for us to give the rainbow someone deserves because we are still holding the storm we thought we already have let go.

One day, I felt so cold and the Earth began to move,
but it couldn't get anywhere near the Asteroids'
Belt. Though it broke me to million pieces, I finally
sensed heat, somehow.

I don't know where you are now,
it's been so long;
and the memory
     of your hair,
     of your eyes,
     of your hands,
     of your waist,
     of your skin,
     of your scent,
     of your dreams—
had long been gone.

Yet, every time I recall the sound of your laugh...
That spontaneous laugh of yours, you know,
I just close my eyes and for a moment,
I would have you all over again.

Wherever you are right now, I wish you are looking at the world smiling and regret nothing. I want you to know that I greatly enjoyed your company more than the fishes to the moon. I won't stop looking up there, especially now that I'm down. You were the heaviest part of my heart and that is why it's difficult to just let go; but I promise I'll continue walking on...

I miss you so much!

"I love you. You know that. You're fully aware of that. Your face and your smile are the things that always arouse me from my bed every single morning and keep me lively throughout the day. Your voice will forever be the music I listen to through my earphones. You are the greatest biological creature that ever existed in my world. And if I ever lose that world, or those earphones or that bed, please, please, don't be mad at me for being careless. Be mad at me, for being impatient."

Several hours after he received her text, a call from her mom came. While sobbing, she said *"She's happy now, wherever she is."* Then he realized what she meant with the word, "impatient."

I tried so many times to write down the love we had
but the paper only gets wet every time I try to. Even
the pillow I put my face on when I lie down on my
bed at night was choking with the tears pouring
down from my eyes with the thought of what's left
for me to enjoy ever since I lost your love. How
lovely the horizon is when the sun is down and how
lonely I felt under this unknown sky? No stars to
accompany my distressed thoughts, just clouds to
make it worse.

I was delighted when you told me one day
of how much you love me
of how much you appreciate my being.
That you are grateful to me for not giving up on you.
And that this relationship
will only end in church someday.

We end, indeed, in church today.
Flowers,
tears,
and sadness
For a relationship in a coffin
collapsed from a series of deafening silences.

I promise I'll stay.
I'll sit on this chair
drinking coffee with the mug
you've bought for me. Through
night and day. Through
the storm and the rain. Through
the windy afternoon and the calm morning.

I'll sip as if I'm kissing your lips.
I'll savor its taste the way I feel
your heart in my hands, beating
slowly than mine every time
you tell me you love me;
and I love you too.

Too bad
you already left.

Travelling fast on that road,
I could feel the cold breath of the trees,
finding their way through my skin.

The last time you hugged me,
there was no heat.

I knew my heart would break
into pieces. The clouds
were just dark red.

"Take care of yourself, and thanks for the love
you've given me even though I can't feel it now
because you've already married someone else."

She said 20 years after they had a time to exchange
messages again.

I thought our bond was so strong that it will endure
all the weather and calamity that may pass through it
like the Egyptian Pyramid did. Until you walked away
and the ancient city—once wondrous—was eaten by
the sand, and that the very bond we had was left in
the wide desert, alone.

We were there. Just a few more steps and we could've already been there. But you decided to go down; and you know what? It felt like I jumped onto the rocky ground a hundred times over. It was the first time I looked at nature with sorrowful eyes. I closed them and never saw myself the same again. I was so lost I fell into the valley of tears that empties into the sea.

You won't ever find me!

A Peak We Have Never Reached.

I'm starting to hate this state of being in pain. I want to be alone, but I couldn't. I shouldn't. I'm scared of those demons that would be coming out of each hole in my skin. They'd pull my soul into nothingness just for them to live. I know am capable of overcoming them, but maybe not today. Those evils are just being born.

"You were never in love with me. You needed me!
You used me!"

"If you knew it already, then why are you telling me
this just now?"

"Because I'm in love with you. I made myself believe
that one day; you'd finally walk with me here. Then I
realized, you're in love with being lost and now, I
have to let you go."

He knew it was wrong to leave her, yet he still did it out of anger and he spoke of words he never should have said. But it is already too late.

She was left in pain. As if bullets were shot right into her heart. She was, then, falling gradually while the recent past, flashing like she was watching a scene from a romantic tragedy film. Her eyes: a million fireflies when she first met him, a catastrophe in her brain. She expected her life would never be the same ever again. Her smile was a scene at the bay; they were walking from the beginning of time 'til the end of the world. Their first fight, tears flowing down the city—crushing the buildings, the monuments—it was just a laugh after all, and they kissed as hunger struck them, a battle for eternity, deep and intensely, consciously shifting. As well, the surprises and the gifts she received.

She blinked slowly as the water conquered her face,
she could see his stare and the love he is all made of.
Until her body touched the ground, "is this the fruit
of it all? We are supposed to proceed, go on; but I'm
here. You said you will never let me go, and yet, I am
here."

Wind was holding her. Soil was rising. The clouds
pitied her. Rain fell.

I knew it.
I knew it since the beginning.
Loving you is the same
as letting you go.

You should love yourself a little bit more. Once you value the gemstone inside of you, you will shine.
I've heard that diamonds are the hardest to break.

I really wanted to make love with you. I would certainly treasure that feeling forever. But I already anticipated that you wouldn't stay for long and I didn't want it to poison my thoughts when you're gone. If you'd come back, I'd like to do it but only once you are sure that you want me whole, not only at times when you are broken.

You're a star.
And with billions
of planets in the galaxy, you
fell for the wrong one.

You were once a river and I was once the sea. I have
given you the water you needed through the clouds
and you have returned them back to me through your
mouth. Such process is natural, yet so great, so
powerful and so sweet that I even tried to pound
every coast in the world with the waves of my joy.
Until I lost the clouds. I lost the clouds. I'm sorry!

I always fear distance...
for sometimes,
it is so

vast that we
might never see each other
again.

I admire you so for reaching this part. I really do! And yes, it's fine. I know what to do. I will understand the situation we are in no matter what. You have much of my favorite songs now, please don't get tired listening to them. As for me, I will keep you in my poems forever.

You only have two lives to live. I still love you but many things have changed. If you go away for the second time, our roads will never cross again. So live it well.

Maybe we are still together in a parallel world,
or yet to meet in another.

We are just moving way too fast here.

I wonder how many times you looked back the minute you moved your feet away from me and the second I closed my eyes and cried because of you.

I loved you.
You felt it.
I loved you!
  That was the best thing
I could ever give you,
But you just left; as if
leaving was the only choice
  you had.

 Artwork by: Alex Aguinaldo

It was so unfair.
She had done everything for him
but after all that happened,
he still left her on her knees,
begging, in rain of tears.

That night,
she was so broken that she could even smell
the flowers people would bring for her
once she's dead.

You know, she specified at the beginning of our very first conversation of what she hates the most; it was for someone to disappear unexpectedly in her life without saying a word. Therefore, I promise myself that I will never leave. Ironic as fuck! She just did, and I have no idea what happened.

I knew this day would come, that I'd be confronted
with the truth that everything was just a game.
Wherein all of the laughs, the unending dates and
kisses and sex, holding hands, adventures, those
sunrises and sunsets, those stargazing, were mere
aftermaths of the happiness of having the company
of each other and not with a deeper meaning. Maybe
I just expected that there's so much gravity on the
moon. But I'll be alright. Oh and thanks, for at
least—in this imaginary love we had—you leave
something real.

Pain.

While you were saying that you don't want to see me anymore, I felt the pictures and love letters were turning into ashes together with the burning woods below your chimney.

"No, I just can't let you go!" She exclaimed. "Why should we stop seeing each other? I did everything I could to make you happy. Have you found someone better than me? Are you tired of loving me? If you're already unhappy with us, just tell me! Don't mind if my heart breaks into pieces. Don't mind if tears fall from my eyes. I want your honesty. I know that suffering is inevitable in love. But I want to know why it hurts a lot!"

She was seeing leaves falling from the branches of a tree, while listening to the apocalyptic sound that was coming out of his mouth.

Every time we fight, I feel like a fisherman in the
midst of an upcoming storm—not knowing whether
I will be eaten by the waves or be able to survive it.

He was singing and dancing like a five-year old kid on his favorite song. She couldn't stop laughing while watching him. At least by doing so, he was making her happy for a while... on her hospital bed. Each day, he performs to cheer her up. But deep inside, he's like a building, battling with an earthquake; constructed to be torn apart piece by piece every single day by looking at her and thinking until when the tube will stay beside her.

Most of the time, our feelings for someone is a mere byproduct of the unending argument among our neurons on reasons why we stumble upon that person, when they are only meant to pass by, and nothing more.

Your absence makes me think of how many people I could meet, know, and fall in love with if I only get up from my bed and travel.

You noticed it the first time,
when his eyes were losing their lights,
when his pen were running out of ink,
that he stopped asking how your day went
and slept without kissing your lips.

You are supposed to wake up
by the time the alarm rings.
Then he'd caress your cheeks
and kiss your forehead.
But now, you are still awake.

It broke my heart when you said
you want to go somewhere else.
In a strange place where no trace of me
could ever remind you.

I was very disappointed that I
couldn't make you stay, that I
could only cry and bleed.
So... there!

I know love is a very complicated thing. I heard it a million times over. It's as complicated as this world. However, I still find my way flying into it. It is wonderful and diverse. But once I crash on a certain field, I can't go back anymore. Because this world gives us a thing and then takes something in return.

Love, indeed, is a mixture of loneliness and happiness. But perhaps, just like this world, once your love is born, it is expected that it will die... eventually.

"Sorry, I just don't want any misunderstanding in the future," she said. "If you want to be friends, I am up with it but I am just really hoping you are not expecting more than that. You know, I am starting to like someone else now, so..."

"Yeah, it's fine," with a high-pitched tone he said brushing off his shoulders.

Feelings just do evaporate over time.

When you've been to so many places
and yet, you are still just friends?
It feels good as much as it hurts.

You want to think that through friendship,
you may last; but you can't deny, on the other hand,
that forever isn't truly long sometimes.

You would just keep on smiling so to hide
every oxygen your heart is failing to take in;
and cry until you'd fall asleep if you can.

You are that weak to confess what you really feel;
and you're that strong to wake up each morning
as if nothing has ever happened.

I fought in battles I haven't started.
I joined wars I didn't declare.
And yes, I won.
I won them all!
But how come every time I fight for myself,
I always end up being alone.

I feel like warriors being slain during the skirmishes,
and then I become the battlefield,
embracing them—
embracing tens of thousands rotten corpses.

In spite of you pushing me towards hell, I still decided to swallow all the flames in this place so you won't suffer once you arrive here.

I'm sorry if I loved you too much. I'm sorry if I thought of you every night even if you didn't want me to. I'm sorry if you can't see the sky now—but promise I wrapped it inside a box to give to you which you never even dared to open. I'm sorry if I held your hand too tightly when you were already holding someone else's, just as strong as mine.

I am just too far away from you
that even at the speed of light,
I'll be long dead
before I ever reach your eyes.

Whenever they ask me about us, about what I am doing, I always tell them that you are like a bookshelf lacking some books and I'm just filling those spaces to make you whole. I feel joy by doing so and should not expect that it will last forever. But then, I fell.

Time passed by, like a knife passing through my heart, feeling the pain in four weeks delayed time because of my damn frozen neurotransmitters!

But I was the one who's really holding the knife... by fooling myself that I am the librarian.

You said that he meant the world to you
but all that he could offer was friendship.

I remember when you were a rose to me,
and I was just a leaf for you.

You came to me like a heavy and rusty ship, travelling at a funeral pace, with wilted flowers decaying on your lonely body. I thought you were the one I was waiting for so long because I felt the sharpness of your flesh when you docked right in my heart. Then I transformed you like a brand new, fully furnished vessel, but you sailed away too fast. It was the worst. Your smoke polluted my soul. Until now.

I don't know what I should call myself. I pushed you to fly up, welcomed you at the ground when you came back as a shattered rocket that failed to launch, and then again helped you to stand. Now, I am so occupied with the hope of you staying with me, but you were intended solely for flying. And when your flight is due once again, I will just be an outstretched hand helping you, and waiting for you till the launching would fail again.

RUNWAY

I'm so happy that you've become the woman that you always wanted to be—a model. You wore different lovely outfits every day. You showed the world real fashion. You gave them new trends. Since then, you always asked for me, for my presence in your every show—to be your runway. After each event, spectators would buy the clothes you've worn because they looked so beautiful on you and you're very much perfect for them. Each of them would praise you and adore you that make you forget you're on the stage.

Then there I was, still the runway, unnoticed by many, forgotten by the one I allowed to walk on me. A runway, which will later be demolished to be built again in another location.

Back in our small town, you told me you just wanted to have a glimpse of the bigger world. So I helped you. But you were overwhelmed it was vast, like the universe. You got infatuated that you went too far—out of reach. And when you looked back at me, I was already as tiny as that of Earth from afar and you couldn't hold me anymore. You don't want to hold me anymore.

I defeated every evil you can't see.
Cleared your path while you're busy
looking at the back repeatedly.
I'm just here but you never
tried to reach the roots of my eyes.

Someday,
I hope someday you'd notice me.

But for now,
I'll be contented with this same state.
Keep you company.
Embrace your thorn-covered body,
even though it pains me,
even though in the end,
it might break me.

We experience a moment at least once in our life that we would wish time jumps two days ahead.

That night, I heard the resounding voice of the wind that frightened the trees and made the clouds cower in fear. A storm was coming according to the news; and I have never been so afraid my whole life, of what tomorrow may bring.

Stop telling me that
I am your world.
Even neuroscientists and philosophers
debate whether
it exists.

I don't know if it's rightful to call you adventurous,
when you're very much eager to climb mountains,
but never do so because you're greatly afraid to fall.

This saddens me.
I am in a bus going to work.

But *you are on a plane,*
going back home.

"So you're telling me that as long as there are clouds, you'll believe that there's still hope? But he's long gone. Don't think too much of him. Look at your eyes! I've never seen blood fall down from the sky for a shallow reason that there are clouds. You should stop seeing him in your mind; it's pointless." Her friend exclaimed.

"I think of you at work, wondering what you are doing at that moment too. Every time I take my lunch, I am also wondering what you are eating. You are my thoughts before I sleep and every morning when I wake up. I don't know why but I always think of you. You can find every bit of you in my mind. You can find every bit of you in every damn part of my life! You are everything to me don't you know that? You are everything to me!"

She looked down sobbing, pressing on her thumb finger, and in a low tone she continued, "But to you, why am I not?"

"You should count the stars tonight," she advised.
"For tomorrow they will gone."

"You're so lovely," he said.

"Thanks! You think he'll like me?"

"Of course he'll do. Why shouldn't he? You're very beautiful..." Then he walked closer to her and whispered, "...and you'll be the most beautiful girl in the place tonight."

She laughed and patted him on the shoulder. "You know what? You really are my best friend."

At the prom, he did nothing but watch her dancing with the guy she had a crush on for a very long time. She was looking at the person the way he was looking at her from the chair at the corner. It was a torture for him; his heart felt as if it bleeds from the inside. If he could only scream, punch the table or himself until the bleeding shifts to his outer parts without anyone noticing.

The music stopped and she sat right next to him. "Ha! I think am the happiest person tonight!"

She looked at him. "What say you?"

He made a deep breath and smiled, "Indeed, you are. I'm so happy for you."

One day,
she will just stop writing about you...

for a reason that you are
no longer a man of your word.

I fear that once I tell you I love you,
you might go.
I wish that time comes
when I'm finally ready to get hurt...
because it's already too late.

RAIN

I don't know how many miles I've gone just for love. Like this water pouring heavily, tilted as if they're trying to reach for something. They've come this far because of the strong wind. They wash the streets; the plants, they ease their thirst. Someday, I'll be as worthy to someone as this.

Sometimes, I am afraid of receiving e-mail attachments. Yet, once I receive one, I'd download it right away and you'd find me smiling at every word written. I enjoy it so much that I want to be those words themselves... than just be the one reading the message. Only to find out that it was actually meant for someone else; was just sent to me accidentally.

NATURAL PHENOMENA

You've known each other
for ages, you were...
You were the Ring of Fire:
that heat between your stares,
the magma flowing inside your veins,
the lava on your shared lips.

The ocean waves, were...
Were always at war on the shore
with the tiny sands, you've spent...
You have spent winters
warmer than the summer forecasts.

How ironic, that is,
you were left in the freezing sun.
The flares, the enormous blood—
clotted and no longer red,
forgetting your lungs to collide
with atoms and molecules

in the atmosphere of your heart.
The bluish Northern lights it brings,
is the only scene you will never watch
as it turns the cardiac muscle into ice.
It's harder to pump.
It hurts. It sucks.

Your hand, against your chest.
This isn't part of your fantasy
of penguins and polar bears
rambling around your skin,
of snow falling in your dreams,
an iceberg to such an innocent ship.

The equator,
it never came in your mind
that it sits right next to the Pole
until the flame stopped burning.
And it doesn't seem
that the climate will change, years
and years after all these.

That
Hurt
us
Both

TROPICAL DEPRESSION

People think it's different.
Like they won't worry as much
because it isn't as fast as a super typhoon.
But it is as cruel!
It stays longer in the place.
Bringing water, the rain—
it damn comes to you
as if you've never loved it before.
Too heavy, that you cry each night
without knowing the clouds.
It's suffocating, it's drowning you.
Each day you'd wish you could swim
yet you just sit on the corner of your dark room
or lie on your bed like it is the softest thing
you could ever rely on.
And you couldn't think of anything that isn't.

The rivers are spilling over red liquid,
flowing everywhere and you,
you can't help digging them on your own
because the government tells you to.
Because for you, it is not that painful as living here.

But life, as you know it, is hard.

And is beautiful too
only if you open your door again a little bit
to let light pass through,
or your window to see the world once more.
You can try.
Don't give up trying.

Tell me you don't miss the old you.
The dream as clear as the night sky at 2 a.m.
You knew there are countless stars out there to reach.
And that you literally can't.
Though, you'd smile even so, because why not—
You can.
You feel because you can.
You think because you can.
You stand because you can.
You live—because you can.

It's okay not to be okay for now.
Having a storm is not a weakness.
It can stay for long but it doesn't mean
that it's the very last thing you could have.
Natural phenomenon or man-made event,
it doesn't matter anymore because like Earth,
we have different weathers here in our mind.
We laugh or we bleed, then they pass.

MAN-MADE EVENTS

Days have passed.
Weeks. Months. Years.
You never expected,
but you made the weather changed.
Heartbeat, there were earthquakes.
Spontaneously. Massively.
Which shattered the crust
then broke the polar caps thousands
and thousands of miles apart.

You know well that Titanic sank in 1912,
that the world progressed dramatically
    since the Ice Age,
and that there are animals which
    just cannot stay longer in one place.
This is the thing that you need,
because this is where your feet
    should really be.

Yes, it feels weird when things
    turn back around.

You breathe because you can.
If you're in the middle of the Earth,
all you have in the sky are clouds.
Norway or the Philippines,
it's just the same.
It depends on how you value
    each moment given.

Because seasons is a cycle—
You'd know what comes next
    based on what and how you feel.
And you'd realize that the sea
    is just as calm as any situation,
if you'd only look at it from a distance.

So here you are now;
not sharing something,
nothing inside,
no between.
You are just the Ring of Fire.
Happy, contented,
and courageous enough to face life.

Forgive those who have hurt you. Each of us has been hurt or have hurt another, once or so. There are people who will come to see you as a setting sun—captivating—that makes them stop by to watch, and then decide to change course and chase after you instead. Your afterglow will inspire them to be with you long enough until they see another one and leave you like you're any other star. Nevertheless, don't loathe them forever. They go for the things they think they need to reach their destination. You can be a part of it, but it doesn't always mean that you'll always will. You are following your own dream too; and once in your life you've also hurt someone else in the process. Somebody leaving will hurt you, of course, but you'll eventually be fine.

So don't be afraid to love again.

I'm not old enough to say this, but probably when you reach the age of 70, you'll look back at the path you've traveled; and the elongated part will dim the messy road you've been through. It was for the reason that you have never stopped loving until you finally found the person who completely believes that sunsets do happen because... you are there.

I never thought I could forget you. It was like an entertainment in the ancient times, in a coliseum where I am battered by weapons I didn't make. All I wanted was for it to end to stop the cheers.

Now, it seems like you happened a thousand and eight hundred years ago.

From a distance, I
saw her tears fell down. Then
there were flashes of lightning, but
I didn't hear her scream.

I could only imagine how heavy
her emotion was. Until
she calmed down. Today,
she is fine.

I know I can let go of you. It is just that, it is always different when you are around. Like when you were looking at the computer screen, then you smiled because you knew I was looking at you; it was precious! It's obvious that I am in love with your beauty. I know it won't last a lifetime but I don't care. I'm still in love with you. I am not in love with the flower, or the stars, or the night because they are kind or whatsoever, but because they are beautiful.

You have your flaws. I have mine. I understand that they are part of our being, and that doesn't make us ugly in front of the person who loves us the most. Nevertheless, I still want to mention it again, that for me, you are a flower that lives in every season, that you are the night stars that stay even in daylight. And if you're happy with what I'm feeling, with what I'm seeing, I will never look away. Forever, I'll stare.

I dreamt I was on a very long flight. I arrived in a different reality, at a different place, with different people. No pain and no worries left in my heart. Still, your existence is frozen in my thoughts—bringing me back to the present.

Even in my unconscious state, you are still my consciousness.

I remember the night when innumerable letters fell from the sky, she wrote *goodbye*. I hated how she turned the page right away while I was still carving *stop*. She's gone, but I didn't give up. I continued writing with hatred and bitterness until I learned how to write *forgiveness*. There are still millions of empty leaves in my book and after a thousand, she came back with an article of sorry and regret.

Yes, I never gave up on her. I love her. Have I not told you yet that she is my paper and my pen? She's the one I ever wanted to end my book with. We went through a lot. We wrote together once and believe me the strokes were intense. We inscribed both weak and powerful words; let them gather in every party, in weddings, in lectures and speeches, in debates, in court, and on the streets.

We are the writers of our own stories, after all. If we're in love with letters, words, and sentences combined, I think there's nothing wrong with writing together again.

Sometimes life confronts us with the dilemma of choosing between two roads. If our mind is telling us that we have to make a choice for us to begin a new life, take the first road. But if our heart is saying don't let go, no matter how strong the brain is, pick the second one. That path will lead us to someone who just left earlier. If we run, there's a chance we could still catch up. What if the person stopped in the middle waiting for us or he/she comes back while we are walking on it? We take chances no matter how slim it may be. We often take risks. It may hurt us badly in the end, but when we love someone that deep, the idea of pain just evaporates.

Tell me all of your mistakes...
and I'll change the questions.

Tell me all your regrets...
and I'll change my decision.

You helped me conquer my fear by looking down from the 23rd floor of a building. By jumping from a 200-meter-high bungee, trusting the rope to hold me 'til the end. By jumping off a plane 12,000 feet above the surface and feel one of the highest joys as a man. Then I've realized that my deepest fear was losing someone. That person who held me day after day while I was trying to look down from floor to floor. The one who never got tired of telling me that I could do it, just jump and feel the nature; and who was holding my hand falling through the air and had me witness the overwhelming beauty of the world beneath us.

I came to that stage of facing it, after all. I fell into pieces. But you taught me of courage, so I jumped again.

Stare.
It's where we started.
It's our foundation.
It's the seed,
and we grew to eternity.

She had these thick and high walls around her when I arrived. Over the years, I conquered her kingdom through diplomacy and marriage.

of everything I ever imagined.

You're the end

I remember the moment I was waiting for you on our wedding day. God said, "Let there be light."

Then you finally showed up, and life formed beautifully ever since, one after another.

I had the greatest feeling. My heart was uncontrollably jumping up and down as if I am under the fireworks on the New Year's Eve. Everyone was smiling, looking at her in her white dress, walking slowly through the aisle on a red carpet, towards me. It felt like I was seeing the Northern Lights for the first time. I could hear angels playing the harp.

"At last, I will be able to hold my eternal life."

"Forever doesn't exist," she said. "I know because I don't see it in your eyes, but the carved word is obvious—lifetime. You are the person I'll spend the rest of my life with. I love you to the farthest those three words can go and can't."

People say that the only constant thing in
this world is change; and it sure came to me when I
met you...

so mnay tihngs hvae chagned scine tehn.

I love the way your fingers dance on the piano. They simply take me back to that scene when we first met, and that all the sound they produce was the exact vibrations I received when the waves of your beauty touched the core of my brain.

Let's go to Taiwan;
we'll light up our love and let it fly
to the sky of our wildest dreams
with thousand other stars
and many thousand souls.

TAKE ME BACK TO 1986

Seeing you only a few days in a year is like catching rain in the Sahara Desert or witnessing someone smile in a funeral procession. Just a few wonderful days with a hot air balloon in my sky, which would be followed right away by the burning fire and the rest would fall down into ashes. **It feels like waiting for the Halley's Comet to pass by the Earth every 75 years.** But I swear to God the minute it crosses before my eyes, I would have it photographed billions of times with each millisecond it moves; in every angle from thousands of cameras I place throughout the landscape… plenty enough for me to admire until the next moment it arrives again.

Wherever I go, I swear I will always go back to you simply because there is no other door which I have memorized every detail, except for this home.

It's fine. We may not share the same bed with every turn of the Earth. We may be sleeping at different time and space. But we will make it. You'll lie down with my sweet "good mornings" and I'll wake up to your motivating "good nights." Our days would turn well no matter how bad they went, or broken they may be. We are going to be like this for long, and save our every "I miss you" so that once we see each other again, it will be more than enough for us to stay together for all the years to come.

If I were a sailor,
you would be my ship.

If I were a merchant,
you would be my gold.

If I were a warrior,
you will be my sword.

Without you,
I am nothing.

And if I ever lose you,
I would consider myself a fool;
perhaps an idiot.

PARADISO

I dreamt of you.
You were singing.
And there I was, floating in the air
listening to the relaxing sound of nature.
Then in every heartbeat,
you were getting prettier and prettier
just like the rose and every flower in the garden
that being there was the same as being in heaven.

Though I don't know what heaven looks like.
But having you, all of you,
your voice,
your Bubble Nebula eyes,
your fluffy cheeks,
your lips that remind me of
the bloody sunset I captured through my lens,
and your face and your skin
as beautiful and as soft as the silk
that Marco Polo introduced to the west;

It seems that, by this time I have reached it.
Until I woke up here,
and you,
in paradise.

A real superhero doesn't wear a mask or a cape. He wears compassion. And he needs someone to be his Mary Jane, or maybe Harley Quinn?

"Would you leave Earth for another world if one appears all of a sudden?" She asked.

"I'm a man of adventure you know that, so literally, yes!"

"Oh." Her forehead creased.

"There are Earth-like planets," he said. "Planets that could support life too, but this Earth has been doing it for a very long time. We might be walking towards turmoil, if not prosperity. Nevertheless, whatever angle I look at it, I still want to be here. So if you would ask me again, and if this is what you meant, my answer is no, figuratively."

She is a Catholic but he is an atheist. Yet, they understand and respect each other's belief. They talk of it in equal and profound ways without fully disagreeing with one another. For love is better than pride, and deep affection is better than a religious argument.

"Have you ever thought if in the past we have already met each other, full of dreams, but had to go on separate ways? And here we are now to fulfill those thoughts and be together forever?" Curiously, he asked her.

Marveled, she said, "No. I'm currently thinking of the future—distant and brutal—when we have all the answers in life and aware of everything that has happened in this world. But one of us died and our soul had to go back here at this very peculiar moment in time and conquer these bodies just for this moment to take place... just to be with each other again."

She's your Cornelia.
She's your Kate Middleton.
She's the Mona Lisa on your wall.
She's your Helen of Troy.
She's your "Mother of Dragons."

He's your Caesar of Rome.
He's your Prince William.
He's the da Vinci of your tomorrow.
He's your Homer in poetry form.
He's your "King in the North."

They became like two heavy entangled chains which are nearly impossible to unbind; which left Cupid scratching his head, wondering if he made a mistake of hitting them tremendously.

I remember the first time I heard you laughed over the phone. You told me you were down and I had a problem of my own. Then you recall something I didn't clearly hear, and you laughed non-stop which made me laugh too. That addicting giggle of yours, it was way therapeutic. Your breath trying to catch up with it and the sound of your voice, they are like the waves and the wind in a duet, and then you'd see the rushing clouds from behind. That scene felt as if I was on the beach—you were just beside me. And with the overflowing joy contrary to our sadness... that's when I knew I will fall for you.

S E A S O N S

I will always be here for you.
Be it spring
when the flowers bloom on our skins.
Be it summer
when the warm wind blows
following our smiles.
Be it fall
when the leaves descend
from trees with our dreams.
And when the winter comes,
forests, lakes,
and cities will be filled by snow.
When the world is as dark
 and as cold as Pluto.
I will bring you the Sun
I will give you my tightest embrace
I will fill your mind with memories
that will last until the next
thousands of years.

I stopped dreaming after
you woke me up,
but the taste of
your kiss
felt like I am still asleep.

NEUTRON

I was so miserable that moment—catastrophic mind, bleeding heart, shattered life. No one could feel me as I sat in camouflaged on one pitch-black side of space. Until I saw her from another corner. Head tilted, pure diamonds were coming out of her eyes. The magnetic field I felt—it was denser. So dense that I talked to her. We've shared our own despairs, how dark approached us, how we lost our radiance, how we ended up at this same state while millions are much brighter than that of the sun. We were two Neutron Stars crashing into each other—creating gravitational waves. And after a hundred and thirty million years, mankind has finally heard of us.

S T A R S

We started from that situation. My light faded away. It was so dark that I had nowhere to go. The density, I sat on somewhere, sobbing. Then I heard a voice. I was trying to send him away. That certain part of the cosmos, it belonged to me——I wanted to be alone. But he just kept talking. He said he's been there, and is still there; that he's not trying to comfort me or make me smile, he just want someone to talk to and said I needed it too. With his desolation, how he became nearly unobservable after a supernova, I presented my own. It somehow dried my tears. His shoulder was not a friend to cry on, but our emptiness was enough to commence the spin. So many spinning before the real collision happened; so many stares, but with that intense gravitational pull, there's no turning back. And, though, our brightness vanished long time ago, doesn't mean we are lost forever. It was a theory from afar at first, but today, we are revolutionary.

With billions and billions of planets in the universe, I
couldn't think of anything more spectacular than the
feeling that we exist here with each other.

It was that time of the night when the storm passing by above their roof, and they were on their bed savoring their burning bodies, sweating from the heat produced by their love and excitement, partly brought by the cool breeze blowing outside the open window. Her hands against his chest, she was being caged in his arm, holding her from the back to limit her in any resistance while the other's caressing her thigh gently. Then he turned his lips on her chin and slowly navigated down to her neck, so slow but intense like that of the heavy rain pouring on the flawless streets. She could feel her hormones going up and down and she couldn't do a thing but close her eyes, feel the heavenly sensation and moan as the thunder roars. It was the best storm so far in their life as a couple and they didn't stop until the last drop of water from the roof fell into the ground.

MAGNETIC FIELD

Happily, we fall off from the clouds of our dreams
Sailing gently in the air we choose to breathe
Into the grounds of endless kissing scene
Down to the bottom of our ego and id.

Falling, is such a fine journey before we find
the right rings. And we're enjoying it
as we have each other's lips. But miles
are the distance from your neck to your legs.
And the sky is in between your arms and your legs.

We are obviously so drunk with the connection
we are sharing. Of all these stars
and comets in the pouring rain. That indescribable
beauty of a galaxy we make in every spin. Locked up
inside a special magnetic field we are in.

Your
lips
ARE
strawberries
FROM
heaven

It is love when your kiss no longer signifies
hunger for just sex; but intimately—with
your softest lips—just as how night
approaches the sky, not that fast but just
right. You'd know what you're about to see
even if you close your eyes.

PLANETARY ALIGNMENT

Two of the most precious things about you that I am so in love with is the way you look at me and then the way you bite your lower right lip before landing me a kiss. It is very tempting and takes me into different psychedelic dimensions this world has never seen. It doesn't stop anything. It makes a thing moves! It's like an unobservable scene where two Great Red Spots joining together giving Jupiter a life to remember. As enthralling as a collision of stars that lights the darkest space in a span of several trillion miles. It is so slow that makes me close my eyes and imagine how time kisses the clock, then it starts; how time kisses everything here on Earth, so we advance. Though Mars said it first, I still want to tell you that your eyes are where I'm lost in. Your kiss is where I'm lost in. I get lost in time that I always do find your place in my better self.

You are but a forest, just uninviting;
So dark, yet I want to embrace.
So untamed, yet I want to be with.

I will love you.
I'll be the wind
that will fill the spaces of such wilderness.
I'll be the wind
that grasps each branch and leaf,
and make the trees whisper my name.

Wolves will howl at night,
as the strong wind
blows beneath the woodlands.
Bushes will grow,
as it catches the raining fire.

Yes, I will love you—day and night.
Send me a bear, a tiger,
or any wild animal you have there.
But I'll still be here
I will love you.
I know, I'll do!

THE AWAKENING

It was after that powerful electricity emerging from your fingertips tapped the strings of my darkened heart, that a song started to play all over my flesh—distorting time and space. For the first time, in a broken and slow motion, I saw my spirit going out of my physical self because of the inviting touch of your soul. I watched them combine as if they both own the seen and unseen world, until our body reached them and the two of us fell to the ground.

Often times, she'd sleep in my eyes and dream on my lips. Her hair is my veins and my arteries; and when she wakes up, she's a radiating ruby I so love to see through my ribs.

YOU ARE MY PAPER AND MY PEN

I'll write again
Of poems full of similes and romanticisms
Of stories full of hidden messages
and surprising twists.
I'll write again
Of everything that I have seen
Of every place that I have been.
I'll write about you and me
Of rain kissing the sea
Of flower feeding a bee
Of wind embracing a tree
Of chain holding a key.
I'll write again
Of how a star fell at night
Of how dark welcomed the light
Of how perfect the moment is
when you are within my sight.
I'll write again
Because you are my paper and my pen
Because you are my heart and my brain
You are my happiness
and my beautiful pain.

G O. H O M E.

Let's travel the whole world together.
Look for a good location in Scandinavia
    and enjoy the Auroras
Then to Louvre Museum in Paris
    and the Eiffel Tower.
Go to Rio
    and visit Christ the Redeemer.
We'll fly to Tokyo
    and have a walk in Akihabara.
Set sail for Caribbean
    under the banner of Captain Barbossa.

I'll be your prince and you'll be my princess
    in front of the altar at Westminster Abbey.
Run for your life as I chase you
    at the busy streets of New York City.
I'll prepare an assault
    and you defend the Great Wall.
You plan a hug
    and I'll kiss you in Seoul.

Take a jump as I catch you
    in Mt. Andes in Peru.
I'll climb the Mt. Everest
    and fall for you.

Let's taste the chocolates of Belgium.
Attend a mass at St. Peter's Basilica
    and explore Rome.
Then back to the country where we belong.
The place we call home.

I could smell your fragrance even at the train station, when I am on the train, or at the mall. Your smell lingers even though you're far away from me. It lingers like the thought of your stare, of your smile, of your face. Though, allergic, I'm drawn to your scent.

At first, you are like this blank paper. I don't know where or how to start, what words I am going to write. I just close my eyes and imagine, let my thoughts travel wherever the energy moves them to. And when I looked back at you, you are already a poem. Then I'm lost again.

I remember on our first date, the moment I tried to hold her hand. It felt like the Earth was falling millions of miles an hour down the bottomless space and when I saw the whole solar system above me, I knew that things will change.

TELESCOPE

I was drowned by the idea
that in my world,
all things are constant.
All things remain the same.
They will always be.
And all that's left for me
is to stare at the stars every night
until I fall asleep into my bed.
Yet you prove to me that love is
not just what's at my very eyes
fancying those tiny little lights above.
But a telescope to reach them
to be with them
and to hold them
forever.

The human brain is a like a universe. Imagine this world has more than 7 billion people, with a series of different realities happening at the same time inside these more than 7 billion independent universes. If multiverse were true, I think they are not parallel at all. They may collide with each other. Maybe they are meant to collide with each other, just as what happened between yours and mine.

I never looked at her as a disaster, but I could hear the frightening sound of bedrocks underneath my chest when the earthquake hits.

"What took you so long?" She asked.

"Doubt."

"Doubt? Uh—" She paused for a moment. "About me?"

"Self-doubt. I thought that you're not going to like me. That I'm not the one you're looking for. I couldn't push myself any further that it made me dream of you. I started seeing you more than a person—a fairytale, an angel. You're so high. Sometimes I imagine our future being happy together. I've come to enjoy these thoughts. But I really wanted you, so I gathered all the courage that I could. I had to think things carefully and thoroughly. I don't want to hurt you in the end just because I have fallen in love with the idea of you in the first place. Then we finally met—heard your voice and your laugh personally, saw your smile, your hair, got to know your hobbies, your fears, your dreams. You were very real since the first time I received your message. It took me so long… I will never leave you!"

It was actually just two days ago
when Big Bang happened.
It's rapidly expanding—
forming galaxies,
forming stars,
forming planets,
forming you
and I in every part of it.

She saw him went out of his tent and put up a mattress in an open space. It's 2 a.m.; it's one of the best moments to watch the sky. They have set camp under the trees after reaching the summit a few hours ago. She couldn't sleep; she was thinking of him. She thought everyone was taking a rest. She watched him as he lied down and stared above. Then she decided to join him. He didn't react.

Time passed by. Breaking the silence, she asked, "Do you think stars truly fall?"

"I think so. If not..." He turned his attention to her, "...then why are you here?"

He's thinking of me, too. Her heart fluttered. She then heard him laugh softly. "I'm just kidding. It's a myth. Stars don't fall." He said.

"I think..." She paused. Then continued, "...one of them is truly falling." In awe, he looked at her again.

And a couple of shooting stars flew across.

I always wanted to meet a painter, or a poet like me, or a psychology or philosophy or physics major, or someone who reads a lot. Because I'm sure they are thinkers, they think widely and deeply. I think that a conversation with them would be no end. So I fancy them.

Then you came. I admit you didn't meet the standards I set the first time we met. But when I saw you again—your whole face, your being—the feeling was like witnessing The Mona Lisa, a 500-year-old piece of art, wrapped in paper and being unraveled before my eyes; a 300-year-old poem being read to me by Shakespeare himself; a creature being perceived by God who still exists even after I blinked. It felt like I was looking at a book about the beauty of life. I didn't try to spark a conversation there, but it's where all this love in the world began.

I fell in love with you because there are parts of you that I like, and there are parts that I don't. Your demons attract mine. Remember when you multiply two negative numbers? Our demons will surely produce angels of different kinds.

I often thought of love as a distraction in reaching my goals. But I don't know why I never felt that way every time I think of you. Something is covering that word and I love staring at you like I am seeing my dreams. I want to reach them one by one while holding you with other hand.

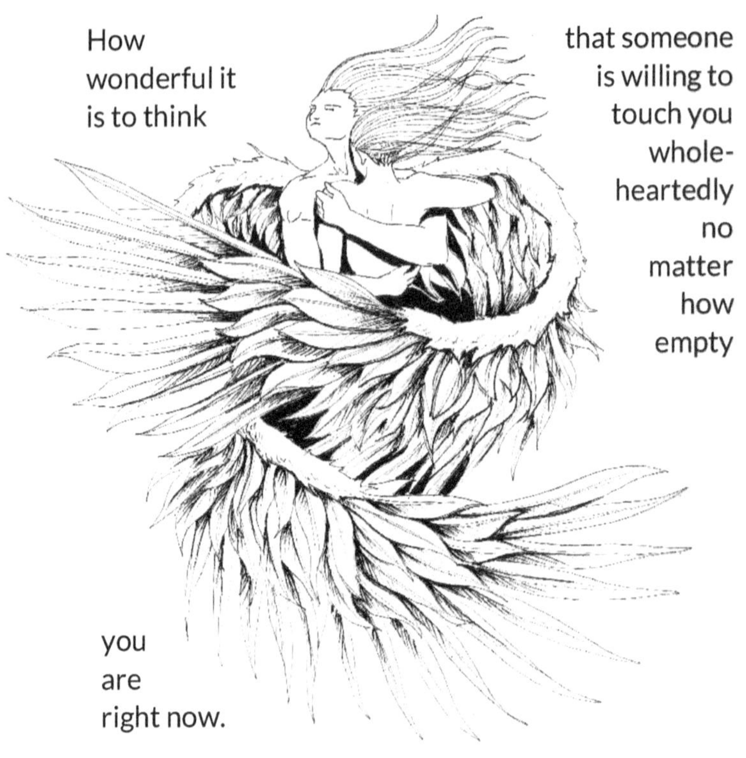

How
wonderful it
is to think

that someone
is willing to
touch you
whole-
heartedly
no
matter
how
empty

you
are
right now.

When I first saw you, I told myself that I have to talk to you. It's like love at first sight but not like you're the Earth possessing gravity so strong that you attract every human being on, but it's the space above that pushed me to come to the surface. I couldn't explain it but I wanted to be with you. It was so great of a desire, which overwhelmed gravity. It doesn't seem like a bed pulling you to lie down on it but it's your desire to rest or to sleep. It doesn't seem like a beer wishing to enter your mouth but it's your desire to drink. And I'm glad that I saw you that particular moment. I'm glad that I approached you. Moreover, I'm glad that my admiration never pushed me to Mercury or to Venus or any other planet but only to Earth; because it's definitely worth it, just being here.

She stopped and calmly asked, "Why? Why are we doing this? Why are you doing this?"

From her left side, he moved and turned himself in front of her, "Because you're an amazing person. You're not just beautiful. You're not just smart. You're not just…" He looked at her downcast but he continued, in an enthusiastic tone, with his hand waving and pointing to her body, "…sexy." He paused and looked back into her eyes, held her chin with his thumb and index finger across, and in a very low voice he said, "You're a goddess to me! You are everything. If I were a farmer, you would be the seeds. There's none in this world that could match the smile that I have as I see my crops grow. And if I have to harvest them earlier before the storm comes, I would, so I won't lose you… because I love you."

And she embraced him.

"Tell me a thing or two about him. Do you feel something for him now?" Her friend asked her.

"He always looks at me like it is the first time he saw me. Sometimes, I'm wondering if there's dirt on my face. Every time we parted ways, I often find myself smiling and feel excited for our next date. Now, all that I remember about him was his stare... and if he's here, he'd smile at me then he'd turn his eyes somewhere, and look in my direction again. What's happening?"

"Girl, he's so in love with you. And you know what? You'll be there too in no time. What the hell is this, I suddenly feel jealous of you."

She laughed. "What? Why? C'mon let's eat... my treat. We have so many things to talk about. I feel like I'm going to explode. I can't contain it anymore."

You see, there is a myriad of words that could sprout out of stars. They are beautiful bodies in heaven. So don't ever complain if I often stare at you. For stars are meant to be gazed upon and they change my perspective in life.

I know, someday, I'm going to be with the person whose path is unparalleled to mine's. Our similarities and differences, happiness and anxieties, thoughts and actions, dreams and memories, will merge all because they are intended to be like Andromeda and the Milky Way Galaxy. But before that unity happens, there will be a long eventful light show, to borrow the words of Neil Tyson—a dance of a half a trillion stars.

EARTHLY BODIES

When I met her at dusk, the clouds
are like burning fire. You could feel it
just by staring at it.
The rays are like guitar strings,
and as the wind blows
the world sings.

From gold
the sky cast a spell,
turned herself into a field
of blooming roses and tulips
as red as our beating heart.
And when Sun was gone
the sea was dark
the atmosphere was black—
we glowed from the ground
that caught the attention of the stars

and made them fall in awe.

We took them each
as the both of us
we're falling in love.

And that those heavenly bodies—
sparkling,
dancing in my palms,
is the very same scene
I see every time
I touch her face.

That's what I do; I romanticize the words I write.
Make it blossom. I don't know how one would react
if I give her a bud but when I offer her a flower, I'm
sure my actions are true and my intentions are clear.
Even if I fail and lose her in the end, I know I will have
my words still.

CURIOSITY

I don't know if I can explain it very well, but I'll describe it to you this way. In every single part of our conversation that she was looking at me, her stare never seemed to reach my irises. It just stops in the middle of the space between us; forming a dense black hole from my perspective.

And it always stuns me; realizing that sometimes, you don't really need to travel so far from home to have a glimpse of an entirely different universe.

There comes a point in our lives when we meet a person who possesses such a defying character that clouds us from our expectations and will change our routine. We'll look at them differently, ignoring others' opinions, and go on as if we're not hearing our friends' voices, as if we never knew our own selves. The more people push them away from our thoughts, the more we think of them. And from the minute we ask ourselves with why's and how's and anything, we are already falling. That little thing we see in them, maybe, is the strongest reason why love was created—because it conquers all.

We heard it frequently that it no longer lingers much in our head, but it's always there in our heart—love conquers all. We know it. We know that if we love a person, we accept them for who they are, because we could sense their true self when people only see the facade. I think love is genuine when we fight for someone without an armor, a sword and a shield, just with our bare hands and from the smallness we first felt for them.

Going back home now,
I think of her—
The curiosity in her eyes
The way she look at the relics
The way she look at things
The minimal reaction she draw on her face
The movement of her lips when she speak.
I fell for all these.
And while she focus her lens into each feature,
I am admiring her detail.

When a museum guide
falls in love with a tourist.

I hope he'd change for you, or for the better. I hope he'd reciprocate everything that you do for him. I hope he'd make you happy again the way he did before.

I know love is giving. But would it still make you happy in the end if you have already given him your whole life and nothing's left on the other side, not even your soul? Would it still be worth it? Of course, you're expecting something in return, maybe not much, but at least something. There will always be a place deep in your heart that is craving for light. Love is not just giving but coexisting and growing up together.

I am not asking you to stop loving him. I already saw it. I admire you for being faithful and positive. But once the time comes where your reality itself is forcing you to leave, I'll give you a dream to start and stay with.

Do you know why I drink? Because it makes me fly; it frees me. I feel unstoppable. I can share much of the thoughts that I only keep at the bottom of my synapses. I become a political analyst, a philosopher, a debater. I engage in metaphysics with anyone other than myself, it's like the only time that thoughts come freely out of my mouth. It drives me to do such things I don't normally do when I'm in control. It makes me, me. And then, I remember the first time I met you.

The best moment in my life
was when I met you.
It was as if I were drowning in petals,
as if it was still Valentine's.
It was like a war
of countless butterflies frozen in time.
Snows were like fires.
It was actually the first time
my mind bowed and kneeled before my heart.
I felt so tense
like a cliff being crushed by the ocean waves,
until I have no other option but to fall.

That day I finally realized why God created Earth,
just so I could describe you with it;
hence, at least, there's a place for us to meet.

So, don't ask me why I never let go of your hand,
because the best moment in my life
was when we met eye to eye
that the whole world reverted back
into the Renaissance.

You told me I should stop seeing you because I would just hurt you in the end. Just like what happens in most relationships, we would finish it like how a meteoroid crashes into the Earth's surface. But that occurrence is normal. Even meteoroids themselves don't worry about their ending, because they know they will end up shooting stars in the dark sky. That is the point of it. We should be after the memories, not the misery.

She is not as strong as my mom, my aunts, my cousins, my sisters or my friends. She is as fragile as an old artifact. But being such is one of the reasons I fell for her. Her fragility makes me want to hold her gently in my ever-clumsy hands.

I'm getting used to it. Grope for your hand instead of my phone first thing in the morning. And instead of checking the time, I wait until you open your eyes. It is the best part of the day, I don't have to worry too much about what's going to happen to the world… because you're already here.

At the beginning, you were nothing to me. I didn't feel anything special for you. Now, I don't know why every time I see your smile, I feel like watching a Harry Potter movie for the very first time.

Imagine you are walking on the street, and then you heard a magical sound like "For the Love of a Princess" being played by someone from a piano. You see several glowing jellyfish dancing calmly when you close your eyes. It is too beautiful you just can't continue with what you do.

I fell in love with you like that. The street was so busy but it became as though a theatre when I saw you.

Once I fall in love, I will do anything for that woman. I may not be the sweetest person in the crowd, but she'll forever exist because my hands won't stop writing about her, my mind won't stop thinking about her. I will always tease her until she's forced to show her cutest look. If she gets mad, I won't stop wooing her until she put her arms around me again. I will make her happy like a sea of flowers in an endless sway of their life because of the never-ending touch of the wind. I won't get tired of doing these because I know it will all be worth it. I'll make sure that I'll be the greatest thing that will ever happen to her and she'll be the greatest poem I'll ever write.

She's an architecture graduate,
and I of history.

If we were a country,
we'd be Egypt
or Greece, perfectly.

I just realized that you're the Helen of this era. Every time I look at your face, I have a glimpse of a thousand ships before me. And when you look back at me, I feel like I'm Troy in burning fire, with all that panic inside. You know, it's like two consecutive occurrences—in one historical epic—happening in reality at the very same moment.

I think I'm in love
with the rain,
with the sunsets,
with the clouds,
with the ocean and the sea,
with the trees,
with the sky,
with the stars,
with the moon,
with the planets,
with the galaxies,
with the space,
with you.

It's obvious.
They are the real wonders of this world
and if one of them disappeared,
I'd wake up from a dream.

R O Y G B I V - Y

The atmosphere could feel the light passing through. Violet. Indigo. Blue. Green. Yellow. Orange. Red. Of all the colors, red travels the fastest. Love is red. It shoots right into my heart I could literally hear the sound, simultaneously. Pushing blood into every organ in my body like it is their very first journey. The vibration. The rhythm. Your existence. With all these colors, you are the only one left I'm waiting to fall. Red. Orange. Yellow. Green. Blue. Indigo. Violet. *You.*

"Do you know the word, forelsket?" She asked.

"Mmm. The," he paused for moment and continued, "euphoria you experience when you are first falling in love?"

"Wow! Yeah. Sort of!"

"Why? You're feeling it now?"

She smiled and blinked for a second. "Don't you?"

I have fallen for you since the ice age, and I still have
my feelings buried in the ground you can never
excavate. It's the unwritten part of history that I am
so eager to tell you about. So please refrain your feet
from walking and just lie down for a moment, to feel
the beating core of the ever lonely soil.

I've never seen a butterfly as beautiful as her.

She walks calmly like a bird flying in the sky: you'd hope your eyes are the only thing in the world she'd perch on.

But she'll look at you like a lioness relaying a message "come closer my deer."

I didn't run. I never ran, because I couldn't. My heart pounded shakenly; it's so heavy I can't walk away.

She's that one who could turn your world upside down. From earth, I fell into heaven I swear!

ONCE THE NIGHT
MEETS THE SEA

I've been in dreams.
I've been to different enchanting places.
I've already traversed a vast ocean.
All because of the thought of you.
And they are all but imagination.
Strange as it is, I love it.
No, I love your voice.
It was actually at that time when you first spoke
that Beethoven was able to compose his 6th symphony.
It's as if my ears first received the sound from a violin
or a bizarre event when I heard a mermaid sing.

You know, you're the spark
of every conversation in my head.
You're the lyrics of my favorite songs
when I listen to them.
If you were the night
I'll be the sea.
You'll realize how beautiful you are
by looking at me.

I'm not a perfect man.
I don't have the luxuries in life and all.
I have my own preoccupations.
But I'll exist for you like oxygen to a human being
or like a table to an elegant porcelain.
I'll be there whenever you need my presence.
You'll have me when the rain become your tears.
And once the night meets the sea,
would you let your stars fall for me?

I can forget these roads I have in mind and turn my feet towards every landscape you'd choose to go to—be it rivers, seas, or mountains in darkness, sunsets or sunrises. For I know that those are fragments to this sole puzzle between you and me.

I wonder if there is such a word on a dictionary about how you feel when you're looking straight into someone's eyes, like they're just her eyes but you're seeing so many extraordinary things in it. Your mind wanders far into the future you've never dreamt of. A dream of possible realities. Because you love her so much that you see her eyes like a camera that records a bizarre movie to be shown years after you've seen the eye-catching, heart-pounding trailer, that is.

I am madly in love with you that I couldn't get mad at
you. There are moments that I wanted to forget you.
I wanted to go away from you and let this feeling
evaporate. Then after just a text or a simple
message, everything's falling again.

Sometimes, I just want to go on a trip at a beach, with my tent and the stars above, to watch the world from afar. I may not have the real me, but at least, I am not inside the reality. Darkness may cover me, but somehow, I am happy. It is heaven when I am one with the nature.

If I were to choose a place where I could build my house, I want it to be on top of a hill with a forest behind. Beside it is a waterfall that produces rainbow every morning, with flowers that would grow all the way down the hill every spring, and a large body of water at the bottom for the universe to lie on. How perfect the home would be if you were with me to watch them.

Be mine
I'll be your coffee at dawn
I'll bring you the horizon at dusk
and you'll become poems at night.

With me
you won't be alone in the end.
Take my hand
and I will never leave.

I could feel her pain by listening to the song she repeatedly listens to. And it hurts. It just hurts thinking how she felt and still feels after he abandoned her like a destructive wave to a ship. She told me that it's already calm as if nothing has happened in the epipelagic zone while she is still sinking down deep towards the abyss.

I have no idea where she currently is, but had it happened close to my island I would definitely catch her, even knowing she'd bring damage to my reefs.

The first time I saw you,
you were holding his arm from the back
same with the way the sea holds the storm.
That moment, I perceived
that there would be a thunder
because a lightning struck.
Until he walked away
and I heard it.
I knew how destructive that calamity would be
and I could not blame him for doing such
and you for doing that. But
I started to hate the rain when
I saw it fell from your eyes.
I didn't approach you just to bathe
nor play, like an 8-year-old child.
I wanted to wipe it out,

and I wiped it out. Then...
and then I started to like the rainbow
when you smiled. Days passed
and I fell in love.

Find me when you're sad. Find me when you feel alone. Find me when you feel haunted. When you're broken and you feel like the Earth revolving in a different orbit, find me. I'll move the Sun and every planet in the system, for you to get back on your path. I'll accompany you like the moon. I'll shine through your nights and bring you tides. I'll make eclipses for you to gaze at. I'll appear in different forms so you have something to ponder on. Sometimes, you might cover yourself with a white cloak, but that's fine, for I know we all have secrets to hide. Together, we can smile before the Yellow Star, or turn back at it to explore the fascinating space through our very eyes. I'm already captured by your gravity and I admire your core and atmospheric beauty. So come to me when you have nowhere to go to. Because the moon will always be there, orbiting from afar—open for any future expeditions.

I spend my nights
thinking further
than reality
and writing
the best words
I could think of.
You see?
I am in love
with words
and sentences,
as you are
with paint.
If I am to be
your painting,
you will be
my poems
and love letters.

Perhaps, you're too far away from me now. But if ever I see you again, I'd thank you. I'd thank you for saving me from myself; for taking my hand when I opened it; for embracing me when I couldn't feel myself anymore; for having me listen to your playlist when I already have emptied mine; for encouraging me to stand and tread on when I already encouraged myself to just lie. When I was seeing vacuum, you carved the universe in my eyes. When I burned my books, you wrote new stories for me to read.

Before, I didn't know that you could mean everything to me. I began to close my hands because I've seen you there. When you're with me, I could sense my soul returning to my body. Of all the sounds, your voice is my favorite tune. I continued walking because you stayed beside me. When you fashion the universe in my eyes, I saw galaxies as I stare at you. I got inspired to read again because of your writing.

I wish I could continue holding you. I promise that my soul will be patient. I promise I will never stop listening to this song. I promise I won't get tired of moving my feet. I will keep this universe forever. I'll finish reading these books no matter what. So once we meet again, I am confident enough to tell you all these and pay you with all my heart. I'll pay you with all my life.

They say that if you look straight into her eyes even just for seconds, you will see the crows resting on the branches of her brain. There are millions of them inside that when you do dare take a small step nearer, you will wake them all and they will end up flying. They are capable of covering the whole world. Days will become nights, and each step you will have to take to get closer to her is years to count; and the stars will only be visible, once you touched her soul.

By then, flowers will begin to bloom from your body and butterflies will start to come out of her heart, millions after millions—to kiss every part of you.

"You know what? I love this place," he said while
looking at the landscape.

"I can see the trees, those flowering plants, buildings,
the people; they're living together like there is a
special connection between them. That's the beauty
in it. They mutually grow."

"And having you here, sitting on the grass tonight
with them, is perfect... more than perfect. I have this
strong sensation inside..." Then he took a deep
breath, slowly turned his head left and looked her in
the eyes "...that you are becoming the place to me.
You are this place to me."

Love her with all your heart.
Don't visit her village just to destroy it after.
You're not a barbarian, are you?
But go there, and make it a city.

You're a fortress obstructing stones from the trebuchets, or a fireball overcoming a castle wall. You are strong either way. So don't fear war, let war fear you.

When you ask him of what she looks like, he would start with: her hair is like lava flowing smoothly down the mouth of a volcano, her bluish eyes are as remarkable as an exploding supernova, her nose is as smooth as an icy mountain every skier would want to glide on, her lips is like a blossoming rose the sun loved to kiss, her face is the very picture he sees in a clear night sky—seductive and heart-throbbing.

Your existence is bluntly telling me that one pen is
not enough to write about you but I need hundreds
of them. If tirelessly thinking of you would lead me to
produce a book, will you read it and keep it, once it's
published?

If I were born some 300 or 400 years ago, I'd be a
pirate. I'd sail on to the high seas: reckless, lawless,
that is—freedom and just pure adventure.
Surrounded by mysteries. Haunted by fellow pirates.
Chased by different governments, as I chase after
gold. However, I was born in this period and I have to
live in it, with law and order inside a society
governed by a few "higher men." Speaking of
adventure; speaking of treasure; at least, this world
has you to chase after.

She got the two greatest skies this Earth has ever possessed, captivating and heart pounding. I focus on them as if I'm looking through an optical instrument, magnifying in so many lovely things that are not visible with the naked eye—twinkling electrical signals. The world stops to let me cherish the moment. Or rather, I'm stunned. I'm not sure what her thoughts are, but I know mine. I'll be sending probes. I'll be constructing larger telescopes.

She's been hurt many times in her life.
She's been badly hurt.
Boy, you have to be patient.
She's been dead long before you've met her.
Decayed.
It's hard for her to trust again.
But time will come where mushrooms
will begin to grow from her body
and open up beautifully to the world,
though, gradually.

So please bear with her.
It will all be worth it,
don't worry.

You know you're in love when your words are slowly
turning into poems, your world is not just evolve
around that one charming sun but as well goes
beyond the solar system every single time.

Nothing can surpass the happiness I felt
at a table while sipping a cup of coffee and
enjoying a croissant while reading
a romance novel at 2:00 A.M. with
the thought of you.

If you were to ask me what's in you that I like the most, it's your relationship with books. I'll always and forever admire a person who reads a lot for I know they think broadly. They think deeply. I won't get bored talking to them because they already have been into different worlds and realities by reading. What I always do look forward to when meeting or talking to a stranger, is a deep and intellectual conversation. And knowing their name would be the last.

If promises
are meant to be broken,
then I promise I won't

fall

for

you

ever.

And after travelling the whole world, he never
thought that he'd see all those marvels fall into one
place upon meeting her.

I wonder
when I will
ever meet
a person
who would
blow
such
clouds
out
of
the
atmosphere

and yet,
make me witness
the
pouring

rain.

Indeed, | 241

The Sweet Words

To Maia, a star in the sky whose beauty radiates from afar. While telescopes are an instrument for reaching celestial bodies, I wrote one.